Tyler
the Tumbleweed
and His Family Adventure

Nick H Roberts

Illustrated by Wayne Mckenzie

ISBN
978-1-957895-47-5 (Paperback)
978-1-957895-46-8 (eBook)

This book is dedicated
to my grandchildren

Jonathan, Kelly, Robert,
Zoey, Hunter, JT, Guy,
Thor, Niko, Alex, Matty,
Katie, Andy, Allison, Neely

And my great grandsons
Francis and Markle
and whoever may come next

I love you all.

One day, Tyler the tumbleweed and his family were talking and just standing around. Well, standing around as far as tumbleweeds can stand, since they do not have legs, you see. There was Roller, his dad, Whirly, his mom, Sticky, his brother, and Scattered, his sister. Sticky was called that because he looked like a pin cushion. Scattered was called that because during the last wind storm she had lost part of herself. Tyler was the smallest of his family but his dad, Roller, had said not to worry, he would grow some day. Scattered complained that she would never find anybody because she had a hole in her middle. Sticky was always trying to find some way of pushing Tyler around with every little gust of wind, which seemed all the time. And since Tyler was the smallest, everyone worried about him, even Sticky.

"Ok," said Roller, "here it comes again," (meaning that the wind had started to gust once more.) "Stay together and hold on!" They would be moving somewhere else today and maybe for the night, but of course, on the desert, one never knew about the winds. Tyler and his family were always at the mercy of the winds. Sometimes they might move inches, then again, they might be moved by feet. Of course, they could also be moved by miles, which was always a big adventure. Tyler had been to a lot of places so far. He had been to the hills, along the river, and by the cactus stands. But somehow he and his family always ended up back at the giant boulder which they called home.

As the wind started to blow, Tyler and his family wondered where they might end up today. Rolling along, they passed others and yelled their hellos and good-byes almost at the same time. That was the way it was sometimes. No time to visit with the neighbors.

Soon the wind started to blow harder and Tyler saw that his family was starting to be stretched farther apart.

"Stay together!" yelled Roller over the wind. But suddenly, Sticky was thrown in another direction.

"Help!" yelled Sticky, as off he went, rolling away.

On they rolled, pushed by the wind. Whirly was pushed away.

"Roller, I love you" she yelled over the wind, and then she, too, was gone. Tyler hoped that the wind would help his mom find his brother Sticky, even if Sticky picked on him.

As the wind kept on blowing, on they rolled; Roller, Scattered and Tyler. Then, as before, away went Scattered, off in the opposite direction.

"Daddy" she yelled, as she was carried away.

Tyler and his dad kept rolling along until a crosswind suddenly hit them. Roller went one way and Tyler went the other as each was separated from the other.

Now Tyler was alone being pushed by the wind. He had never been alone before. His family was always around him.

He wondered where his family was and when he would see them again. The wind started to slack off and Tyler was slowing to a stop. Alone and sad, Tyler started to sob. He missed his family and was a little scared. Since the wind had stopped, Tyler was left to wonder if he would ever see his family again. He knew that if the winds did not blow he was stranded where he was.

There was no one to talk to, no family for comfort, no one to even pick on him like Sticky did.

As he looked around the sun started to set and it was growing cold, but all he could think about was his family.

It was going to be a long night. It had been some time since he slept alone. As hard as he tried, Tyler could just not sleep for very long. All night long the sound of the desert kept him awake.

In the meantime, Sticky had been blown into a cactus patch and become stuck to one standing by itself.

"Well what do you want?" the cactus said.

"It seems that the wind has stuck me to you. My name is Sticky. What's yours?"

"Well, if you must know, it's Ralph, and I like being alone. So if you don't mind you can let go anytime and leave."

"Sorry Ralph. I would if I could, but it seems that I can not move. And until the winds blow again we will just have to deal with each other."

"Well, I do not like it!" said Ralph. And with that neither one said another word for the rest of the night.

Whirly had been blown to one of the very few water holes that appeared in the desert. The wind blew her to the edge, where she got stuck in the mud. As the winds stopped for the night, a road runner came and rested under her for the night. The next morning, Whirly said hello.

"Hello", answered the roadrunner.

"My name is Whirly. What's yours, please?"

"Oh, my name is George."

"Well, can you help me?" asked Whirly?

"Help what?" replied the roadrunner.

"Well, as you can see, I happen to be stuck in the mud and would like to be free."

"I am not sure I can help", said George, "but I will try." And with that the roadrunner started to scratch and scratch at the mud. Slowly, inch by inch, Whirly became free. As a light breeze came up, Whirly moved and then moved some more.

"I think its working," she yelled at George, as the roadrunner kept on scratching at the mud. Then she was free.

"Thank you," said Whirly as she started to move away. "If you are ever near the giant boulder you can have the bugs that are caught in my branches."

"Thank you. I will remember that," said George, as Whirly rolled away once more.

Scattered had been blown away from her dad and brother. She did not know where she was headed, but she hoped it was back home. She did not want to think that she might lose another part of herself again, or worse. What if the wind blew her all apart and she never saw her family again? As the winds slowly stopped and Scattered blew to a stop, she started to sob. She was alone in the middle of nowhere.

As the early dawn began to lighten the morning sky, a gentle breeze once more stirred. Tyler began to move once more. He wondered if today his family would appear. Slowly the wind picked up force and Tyler rolled faster and faster. Everything was a blur. It looked like he was headed to the hills. The winds there could be mean and harsh.

Near the hills the winds softly lightened and Tyler rolled to a stop near a small clump of rocks. Waiting for the winds to pick up and move him again, Tyler saw something in the sand near him move. It looked like a stick, but one end was bent.

Then, there it was, a long brown snake with a bent tail.

"Hi," Tyler said. "My name's Tyler. What's yours?"

"Ssslides my name," the snake said. Slide was a sidewinder with a limp. The limp was caused by a hawk that broke his tail trying to eat him.

"That'sss Sssid over there," Slide said as he turned his head to point. Then Tyler saw the other snake also.

SID was a rattler, brown with black diamonds on his back.

"Hi Sid," Tyler said. Sid just kind of nodded. "Can we be friends?" Tyler asked?

"Sssorry, no," they said. "It is time to sssleep before it getsss too hot usss."

And they both started for some cracks in the clump of rocks.

"Bye," Tyler said.

"Sssooo long," Sid and Slide said as they disappeared into the rocks.

Once more Tyler was all alone. He was worried about his family and wondered where they could be. When Roller and Tyler had been blown apart, Roller was a little worried about Tyler as he had never been alone before and because he was smaller than the rest of the family.

On Roller was pushed, suddenly frightened that he might never see his family again, because up ahead was the river and he was headed straight for it! Then, at what seemed like the last minute, a crosswind hit him, and he was blown away in another direction. But when the winds finally slowed down, and ROLLER came to a stop, he found himself home once more.

Now if only the rest of the family could somehow make it home, he thought.

With the help of George, Whirly was free. The winds started blowing her, racing her over the sands once more.

She still worried about her family. She was thrown this way and that as onward she was pushed. When the winds finally started to slow down, she saw the giant boulder, and there was Roller, too. And when the breeze stopped it had pushed her right into him. That's as close to a hug as you can get for tumbleweeds. She was finally home.

It had been a sleepless night for Sticky. All night long Ralph continued to complain about unwanted company.

When the sun came up once again, Ralph started in on Sticky.

"What! Are you still here? I had thought that maybe it was a bad dream."

"Well guess what?" Sticky said. "You are no picnic either! No wonder you are alone. You can not say anything nice to anyone.

As soon as the wind blows me free you will be rid of me.

"Not soon enough," Ralph replied

After just saying that, a huge gust of wind rocked them both sideways, and Sticky was free, being blown across the sands once more, zinging and pinging so hard that it was making him dizzy. As the winds rushed him over the sands he wondered where his family was and if they were ok. When the winds started to slow down he thought that he saw the giant boulder up ahead. And when the winds finally stopped there was his dad and mom. Sticky was back home safe.

Scattered awoke all alone once more. Looking around she could see nothing as the sun's rays lit up everything around her. Once more she started to sob. She wanted her family to appear. A gentle breeze started to rock her back and forth just like a baby. When she stopped crying, the winds became stronger.

"Here we go again", she thought. With the winds getting stronger they sometimes just bounced her into the air then to the ground then back into the air once more.

"If this keeps up," she thought, "there might not be anything left of me!"

The winds blew her past a cactus patch. She hoped that they did not blow her into them as she would never get out then. But no, on she was pushed, faster and faster, over the sands. And as the winds died down she saw the giant boulder up ahead and as she got closer, there was her family; Roller her dad, Whirly her mom, and Sticky her older brother.

She rolled to a stop. She was home. But where, she wondered, Tyler, her little brother?

As Tyler watched the snakes disappear, he wondered if he would see his family again. It was mid-day with very little wind movement. All Tyler could do was wait and hope the wind would start blowing soon. No sooner had he thought that, a gust of wind hit him. It threw him against the rocks so hard he thought that he would break apart. But no, he was still in one piece but being pushed into the rocks once more!

When the next gust of wind hit him it threw him into the air and over the rocks. Once again he was being blown over the sands. Since he was smaller than the rest of his family the winds seemed to blow harder. Being pushed and racing over the sands, Tyler could only hope he would see his family soon. He had been very lonely since he had been separated from them. He even missed Sticky picking on him!

The winds pushed him onward past a cactus patch, past a mud hole, and even past the river in the distance.

Onward he rolled, faster and faster. Then the winds started to lighten up. Ahead Tyler thought that he saw the giant boulder.

As the winds continued to slow, Tyler saw that he was home. He saw his whole family there; Roller, Whirly, Sticky, and Scattered.

And when the winds finally stopped he was in the middle of all of them, all laughing and crying. The whole family was safe and at home.

They all shared what had happened to them on their family adventure.

And as a little breeze blew past them all,

Sticky once more pushed into Tyler, and Tyler just smiled. It was good to be home!

www.ingramcontent.com/pod-product-compliance
Lightning Source LLC
Chambersburg PA
CBHW080919190726
48293CB00011B/2692